WALT DISNEY'S
The Wizards' Duel

Told by CARL MEMLING

Based on the Walt Disney motion picture,
"The Sword in the Stone"

Suggested by the original story,
"The Sword in the Stone," by T. H. White

Pictures by the WALT DISNEY STUDIO
adapted by AL WHITE and HAWLEY PRATT

GOLDEN PRESS

ONCE there was a boy named Arthur, but every-
body called him Wart.

One day he saw some birds flash by the window.

The birds frisked about gaily in the sunshine—
but poor Wart had to stay inside the dark tower
and study his lessons. He gave a deep sigh.

"Wart," said Merlin, who was his teacher, "whatever you learn, learn as well as you can. Get back
to your lessons, boy."

Wart said, "I wish I were a bird."

Now Merlin was a wizard and good
at changing people into different
things. "I think I'll grant
your wish," he said.
Merlin stood up and, pointing
his wand at the boy,
chanted a magic spell.
At once Wart
began to shrink.
He grew smaller
and smaller
and
smaller.

And suddenly he changed into a little sparrow! His arms were feathered wings. His body was tiny and covered with gray and brown feathers. And he had a squeaky, bird-like voice with which to sing and chirp.

"I'm a bird!"
chirped Wart.
   His tiny body shook
with joy.
   "I'm a bird! Watch me fly!"
   With that he launched
himself from the tower
window. And, with widespread
wings, he glided smoothly
through the air.

Wart taught himself many more flying tricks. Soon he was a swift and graceful flyer.

He was flying along, admiring the clouds, when a black speck showed in the sky. It was a hungry hawk.

"Wart!" cried Merlin from below. "Watch out!"

With a flick of his wings, Wart darted away.
The hawk followed him, its huge, dark
wings beating strongly. It was a long, long chase.

But the feeble little sparrow escaped
by dropping down a chimney.

Exhausted, he fell to the bottom of a cold and sooty fireplace. "Where am I?" he wondered.

Just then he saw a funny old witch peering at him.

"Well, look who's come to visit Madam Mim," she cackled. "A little sparrow!"

"Oh, please. I'm really a boy," chirped Wart. "Merlin changed me with his wonderful magic."

At this the old witch shrieked with laughter.

"Merlin's magic is dreary and dim—when compared to the magic of Madam Mim!" she said. Just then, the witch heard her name called. "Who's that?" she cried.

In a puff of smoke stood Merlin.

"Madam Mim," he said, terribly stern, "let Wart go."

The witch gave a gurgling laugh. "Try to make me, dear," she said. "I challenge you to a Wizards' Duel, to take place immediately!"

Nodding grimly, Merlin accepted the witch's challenge. Soon they were outside and ready to duel.

Wart sat down on a tree limb, and gave a puzzled chirp. "What's a Wizards' Duel?" he wondered.

Merlin answered him. "Madam Mim and I will change ourselves to different things in order to destroy each other."

When Wart heard this he began to shiver.
Meanwhile Madam Mim and Merlin had drawn
their wands.

"Ready," howled the witch.

"Get set..."

"Duel!"

Madam Mim started the duel by changing into a crocodile.

In a flash Merlin became a tiny turtle and hid inside his hat.

And when the crocodile found him there, Merlin changed into a rabbit and nimbly hopped away.

Changing into a fox, the witch chased the rabbit.

But then Merlin changed . . .

...into a hunting dog,

and *he* chased the fox!

Madam Mim changed from fox to tiger, only to find that the dog had changed into a sharp-clawed crab.

Furious at having her nose pinched, she turned into . . .

. . . a sharp-horned rhino!

As a mouse, however, Merlin easily slipped by the lumbering rhino.

But then, calling on her blackest magic, Madam Mim changed into a fearsome, flame-spewing dragon.

Wart gulped with dismay.

What ever could poor Merlin change to now to
save himself?

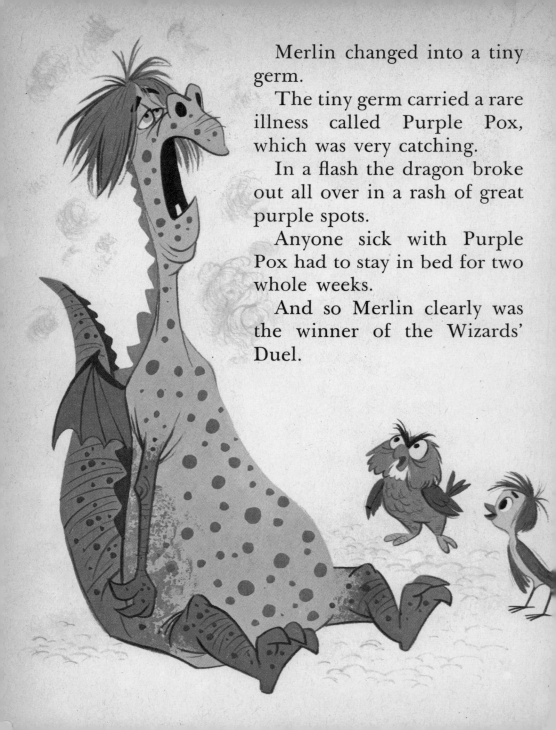

Merlin changed into a tiny germ.

The tiny germ carried a rare illness called Purple Pox, which was very catching.

In a flash the dragon broke out all over in a rash of great purple spots.

Anyone sick with Purple Pox had to stay in bed for two whole weeks.

And so Merlin clearly was the winner of the Wizards' Duel.

Quickly Merlin changed himself and Wart back into people.

"Sir," Wart asked him after they had put Madam Mim to bed, "how did you ever learn such powerful wizardry?"

"When I was a boy," answered Merlin, "whatever I learned, I learned as well as I could."

"Oh," said Wart in a small voice.

Merlin chucked him under the chin. "Wart," he said fondly, "get back to your lessons."

"I will, sir," said Wart. "I will!"

And he did!